IBRAHIM

by Francesc Sales

Illustrated by Eulàlia Sariola

Translated from the Catalan by Marc Simont

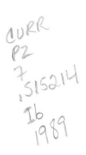

J. B. LIPPINCOTT   NEW YORK

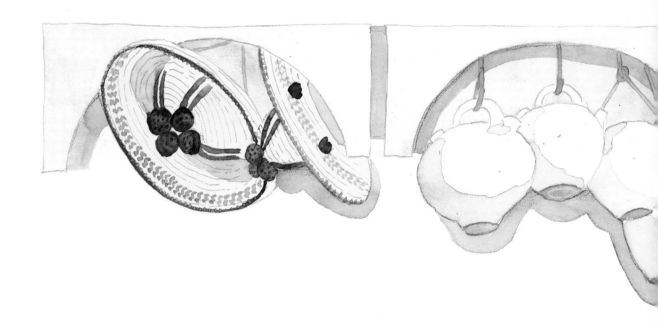

Ibrahim felt good as he walked with his father, Abdul, to the old marketplace in Marrakesh.

He had been there many times, running and playing with his friends, but today was different. Today he was going to work in his father's stall, and the money he would earn would be a first step toward independence and the world of grown-ups.

2

Ibrahim helped his father set up the stall by stringing bunches of herbs and spices and putting out sacks of flour and ground pepper. Ibrahim felt a sense of responsibility and pride as he tended to customers—weighing, wrapping, and making change.

After a morning of brisk business, things quieted down. Ibrahim sat watching the crowd go by when he spotted his friend Hassan.

"Father," said Ibrahim. "Would it be all right if I went off with Hassan for a little while?"

"Yes, of course," said Abdul. "You deserve a break. Go, show our marketplace to your friend, but don't be too long. You never know with business. One moment it's quiet, then everybody comes at once."

"Thank you, Father. I won't be long."

The two friends wandered about the market. They stopped to look at potters, weavers, dyers, and other craftsmen. The market was swarming with activity and ringing with the cries of vendors. Ibrahim felt proud to be a part of it.

They had stopped at a basket weaver's stall when Hassan said, "I have something important to tell you, Ibrahim."

"What is it?"

"It's hard for me to say it, because I see you are very content working at your father's trade and I don't want to hurt your feelings."

"Tell me, Hassan! Now you have made me curious."

"All right, Ibrahim, I'll tell you. I have decided to go to the mountains and beyond to the desert. Always to be on the move, like the nomads. If I stay here, I will shrivel up. I can't stand it. I hate the city."

Ibrahim was stunned. "But you have always lived in Marrakesh," he said. "Wouldn't you be homesick?"

"No, never," said Hassan. "I'm like a bird in a cage here. I could never do what you're doing—spend the rest of my life behind a counter."

"I don't understand you," said Ibrahim. "It's great working in my father's stall, and the market is a wonderful place."

Even as he spoke, Ibrahim felt a strange uneasiness come over him. The words "spend the rest of my life behind a counter" stuck in his mind.

"All right," said Ibrahim after a pause. "Promise you'll let me know how you make out."

"Sure," said Hassan. "I still have to speak to my father, and I don't know what he'll say. But my mind is made up, no matter what. You know what I mean, Ibrahim?"

Ibrahim knew very well what he meant, and the uneasiness he had felt was growing stronger.

When Ibrahim returned to the stall, Abdul noticed something was not right with his son.

"Rest awhile, Ibrahim," he said. "I realize the strain you are under on your first day of work."

That night when Ibrahim went to sleep, tired from the day's work and haunted by his conversation with Hassan, he had a dream.

In his dream some men mounted on camels were outside his window calling his name. He asked them not to shout or they would wake his parents, but they paid no attention.

"Ibrahim!" they kept calling. "Come, leave your house and your parents and follow us."

"Where are you going?" he asked doubtfully.

"Never mind where—just do as you're told. Come on, let's not waste any more time. We're in a hurry."

Ibrahim jumped out of bed and followed the riders.
They rode long and far and over the mountains, until
they came to a vast open space. The moon and
millions of stars spread their light on a carpet of sand
stretching as far as the eye could see.

"We are here, Ibrahim. This is the desert; this is your freedom! What do you think?"

Ibrahim had never seen anything so beautiful. He was so attracted to the desert, he felt he belonged there. He lay there through the night under a sky filled with shimmering stars that seemed to be calling him.

At daybreak the riders came back, but they could not find Ibrahim because during the night he had turned into a star.

He looked down on them as he faded away before
the rays of the rising sun.

The morning after his dream Ibrahim was back at the stall, where he worked steadily until midmorning.

"Father," he said, "I need to rest awhile."

"Do as you like," said Abdul. "You know how pleased I am with you. But there is one thing I wish you would tell me, my son. You seem a little restless, and I would like to know the reason, if there is one."

"It's nothing, Father—don't worry. I'll be all right."

"As you wish, my son. You know you can confide in me."

In the days that followed, Ibrahim would at times be cheerful and hardworking; other times he was sad and brooding.

His dream had shown him the freedom of the desert, and what to him had always been the wonderful marketplace was now beginning to look more like a prison.

The time would come when he would have to decide between the two.

One day, mustering his courage, he went to Abdul and said, "Father, I would like to talk to you about something that's been worrying me."

"Tell me, my son."

Ibrahim told his father all about the problem he was facing.

Abdul couldn't understand how Ibrahim got such ideas. The family had always lived in the city, and Ibrahim couldn't know what he was talking about when he spoke of the freedom of the desert.

"The truth is," said Abdul, "you couldn't endure the hard life of the nomads. You would die of loneliness, and your mother and I would die of sorrow."

Ibrahim felt helpless and frustrated. One day, lost in his thoughts, he accidentally knocked over a sack of red pepper. As Abdul was lamenting his son's clumsiness, Hassan stopped by and asked Abdul, very politely, if he would let Ibrahim go with him for a little while.

"Do what you like," said Abdul, "but don't be too long. I don't know what's come over Ibrahim. Try to cheer him up, Hassan."

Hassan had come to tell his friend that his dream had come true. He was leaving with his uncle, who was returning to the mountains and his flocks, as many in his family had done before him.

Ibrahim wanted to share the good news with his friend, but there was a lump in his throat, and the words wouldn't come out.

"What is it?" asked Hassan. "Aren't you glad for me?"

"Oh yes, I'm very glad. Truly I am," said Ibrahim, forcing a smile.

Hassan guessed what was going through Ibrahim's mind. "I'll talk to my uncle," he said. "Maybe you can come with us."

"No, don't, Hassan. I'm grateful, but I can't. My parents have only me, and if I left them it would break their hearts."

The day was very hot, and the two friends decided to go for a swim in the river.

Diving and splashing in the cool water, Ibrahim began to feel better.

"I should just enjoy moments like these," he thought, "and stop worrying about problems that have no solution."

The next day, Ibrahim was napping by the well in the courtyard of his house when he had another dream.

This time, however, the dream was so mixed up with the real world that he actually dreamed he was asleep by the well in the courtyard of his house.

A genie had come out of the well and was shaking him gently.

"Wake up, Ibrahim, and listen to me."

"Who are you?" asked Ibrahim, opening his eyes.

"I am the genie of the well."

"Don't make me laugh. Genies only exist in the stories Grandfather used to tell."

"But I really am the genie of the well," the genie insisted. "And furthermore, it isn't funny to be told I don't exist while I'm speaking to you."

"All right, genie, all right," said Ibrahim. "Say your piece and let me sleep."

"I know you're upset because you can't go to the mountains and the desert," said the genie, "and you think Hassan has all the luck and you're very unfortunate. I also know that today you decided to stop thinking about your hopeless problems. I know all those things and a lot more."

"All you're saying," said Ibrahim, "is you know a lot about me, that's all."

"Don't be so impatient, Ibrahim. Do you think I would have taken the trouble to talk to you if I didn't have the solution to your problems?"

Ibrahim was growing weary. "Go away and let me sleep, genie, or whoever you are. I know there's no solution and all you can tell me will be empty words."

"Sometimes I think the work of a genie is a thankless task. Here I am showing concern for you and you don't even want to listen."

"All right, don't get upset. Tell me your solution."

"Listen well, Ibrahim, to two things: first, freedom is something you carry in your heart; and second, dreams can also set you free."

Having said this, the genie vanished back into the well.

Ibrahim awoke with a start.

"What's the matter, son? What is it?" his mother asked.

"It's nothing, Mother. I'll be all right."

In the days that followed, Ibrahim could not get the genie out of his mind.

"Whether this business of genies is true or not," he thought, "I'm beginning to think what he said makes a lot of sense."

Every day Ibrahim went to the market, and each day he felt better about his work. In his spare time he enjoyed thinking up stories, recalling adventures he had heard about or folktales he remembered from his grandfather.

Abdul was happy to see the change in his son, who no longer seemed to be laboring under the weight of a great sorrow.

It was a joyful day when Ibrahim went to his parents and said, "From now on you'll always see me happy, because I have decided to live by the words of the genie of the well."

Many years have passed. Ibrahim sits in the stall at the market in Marrakesh surrounded by admiring children who listen to his stories about stars and ghosts.

"Ibrahim knows more stories than anyone in Morocco," the children say. "We could stay here and listen to him forever."

Ibrahim beams and says, "And now, if you're nice and quiet, I will tell you the story of the boy who wanted to run away to the desert, and the genie of the well."

Translator's Note

I grew up in Barcelona, and the first stories I can remember were told to me in Catalan by my grandfather. Sixty-odd years later, at the Bologna Children's Book Fair of 1984, I was impressed with the variety, quantity, and quality of publications in the Catalan display.

I was especially taken with *Ibrahim*, in which writer Francesc Sales and watercolorist Eulàlia Sariola merged their talents to tell a touching story of the ultimate peace treaty—the one we make with ourselves.

Marc Simont

Ibrahim
Copyright © Francesc Sales, Eulàlia Sariola and La Galera, S.A. Editorial, 1984
Translation copyright © 1989 by Marc Simont
First published in Spain in the Catalan language by La Galera, S.A. Editorial, Barcelona
All rights reserved. No part of this book may be
used or reproduced in any manner whatsoever without
written permission except in the case of brief quotations
embodied in critical articles and reviews. Printed in
the United States of America. For information address
J. B. Lippincott Junior Books, 10 East 53rd Street,
New York, N.Y. 10022. Published simultaneously in
Canada by Fitzhenry & Whiteside Limited, Toronto.
Typography by Pat Tobin
10 9 8 7 6 5 4 3 2 1
First American Edition

Library of Congress Cataloging-in-Publication Data
Sales, Francesc d'A.
  Ibrahim / by Francesc Sales ; illustrated by Eulàlia Sariola ;
translated by Marc Simont. — 1st American ed.
     p.   cm.
  Summary: Ibrahim is tempted to exchange his job in the old market
place in Marrakesh for a freer life as a desert nomad, until a dream
shows him that freedom is something carried in the heart.
  ISBN 0-397-32146-5 : $
  ISBN 0-397-32147-3 (lib. bdg.) : $
  [1. Marrakesh (Morocco)—Fiction.]   I. Sariola, Eulàlia, ill.   II. Title.
PZ7.S15214Ib 1989   87-29382
[E]—dc19   CIP
                                                                      AC